Ernie Gets Lost

By Liza Alexander • Illustrated by Tom Cooke

Featuring JIM HENSON'S SESAME STREET MUPPETS

A SESAME STREET / GOLDEN PRESS BOOK
Published by Western Publishing Company, Inc. in conjunction with Children's Television Workshop

"Maria," said Ernie, "I still haven't found a special present for Bert's birthday."

Ernie had been saving up for weeks, and he had lots of ideas.

"I know just the place," said Maria. "Let's go to the P.C. Nickles Department Store."

While they were waiting at the bus stop, Maria said,
"Nickles is a big store, Ernie. When we get there, stay
close to me."

"Don't worry, Maria," said Ernie. "I know what to do
in a store. I go to Hooper's Store every day."

On the bus, Ernie sat by the window.

"Nickles is much bigger than Hooper's Store or anything else on Sesame Street," said Maria. "If we get separated, don't wander around. Look for a salesperson behind a counter. Tell her your name, and that you're lost. And give her this card. It has our names and address and phone number."

"Okay, Maria," said Ernie, stuffing the card into his pocket. "Look, there's Nickles!"

Ernie and Maria pushed through the revolving doors at the store's main entrance.

"This sure is a big store!" Ernie said. He could hardly stand still. Maria held his hand tightly as she looked at the store directory.

"Oh, boy!" Ernie said. "Can we ride on the escalator?"

"Sure we can, Ern. We're going to the third floor," said Maria.

"One, two, three, *step*!" said Maria as they stepped onto the escalator. "Now remember, Ernie. If you can't find me, don't wander around."

"Okay," said Ernie. "Look at all those cookie jars! Too bad Cookie Monster isn't here!"

When Ernie and Maria stepped off the escalator,
aisles stretched out in every direction.
"This way, Ern," said Maria.

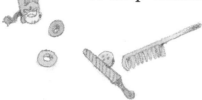

Suddenly a man bumped into Maria, and she dropped her purse. Her wallet, change purse, comb, and everything else scattered all over the floor. Maria scrambled to pick up her things.

"I'm terribly sorry," said the man. He stooped down to help Maria.

Ernie looked around at the colorful displays. "That looks like Rubber Duckie!" he said.

Ernie ran down the aisle to look closely. But it was only yellow soap.

Ernie turned back to where he left Maria. He thought
he saw her going up the escalator, and he jumped on
behind her.

She got off the escalator and walked away very fast. Ernie had to run to catch up with her. When she stopped to look at something, Ernie grabbed her hand. She turned around.

"Whoops!" said Ernie, backing away. "I thought you were my friend Maria." But it was only someone who looked like Maria.

Ernie looked around. The big store seemed more crowded than ever. "Maria's just gotten herself a little lost," Ernie thought. "I bet she's trying to find me right now. I'd better look for her."

When Maria had gathered her things, she looked up
and saw that Ernie was gone. "Oh, no!" she said.
"Where can he be?" And she began to search for him.

Ernie walked down one aisle, then up another. There were lots of grown-ups everywhere, but none of them was Maria.

"There are a million different places in this store where Maria could be," thought Ernie. The store seemed to get bigger and bigger. Ernie's throat went dry.

Ernie realized that he had been wandering around for a long time. "Oh, no!" he thought. "That's what Maria told me *not* to do!" Ernie felt horrible.

He sat down. His tummy felt like a stone. "I'm never going to find Maria now," he thought, and he began to cry.

Ernie reached into his pocket for a hankie, and found the card Maria had given him. He dug it out and looked at it.

"Maria gave me this in case I got lost," Ernie said to himself. "But what was I supposed to do with it?"

Then Ernie remembered. "She told me to find a salesperson to help me."

Ernie looked up and saw a salesperson behind a counter. He jumped up and ran over to her. "My name is Ernie," he said, "and I'm lost. I can't find my friend Maria." Then Ernie gave her the card to read.

"Don't worry, Ernie," said the salesperson. "We'll find Maria for you right away." She picked up a telephone that was behind the counter. "Stay right here with me while we page Maria over the loudspeaker."

The salesperson helped Ernie up onto the counter, where he sat while they waited. "What's taking Maria so long?" Ernie asked. "Did she go back to Sesame Street without me? I'll never find Sesame Street without Maria!"

Then he heard the announcement over the loudspeaker: "MARIA. Please find your friend Ernie in the umbrella department, third floor." Ernie felt a little better.

It wasn't long before Maria came running down the aisle. "Ernie!" she shouted. "There you are!" Maria gave Ernie a big hug. "I'm so happy to see you."

Ernie burst into tears again. "Are you mad at me?" he asked. "I forgot what you told me, and I got lost."

"No, I'm not angry," said Maria. "I'm glad that I could find you because of what you *did* remember."

Ernie wiped his eyes. He felt a lot better now. "I found that salesperson you told me about," he said. "I hope you weren't too scared when you were lost."

Ernie and Maria thanked the salesperson. "Now, Ernie," said Maria, "let's do our shopping!"

After all their wanderings, it was easy for Ernie and Maria to find the toy department. Ernie bought a Pigeon Land game. He knew it was just what Bert wanted.

When Ernie and Maria got back to Sesame Street,
Bert was waiting for them. "Where were you guys?" he
asked. "I was beginning to think you were lost!"
"We were shopping for a surprise for you," said Ernie.
"Happy birthday, old buddy!"